Copyright

My Teacher Doesn't Like Me
Copyright © 2024 by Megan Daly

All rights reserved.
No part of this publication may be reproduced, distributed,
or transmitted in any form or by any means, including photocopying,
recording, or other electronic or mechanical methods without
the prior written permission of the publisher.

ISBN: 979-8-218-38421-0

My Teacher Doesn't Like Me

I dedicate this book to my family.

Another day of school,
and I just don't want to go.
My teacher doesn't like me,
and I'll tell you how I know.

I find it hard to sit still
and keep quiet all day.
I get anxious and hyper.
What can I say?

I walk into the classroom.
A new week has begun.
All my classmates are working.
Shouldn't school be fun?

My teacher tells me to sit
and to please start my work.
I head to my chair,
roll my eyes, and I smirk.

Morning meeting begins,
and I sit with my class.
When it's my turn to speak,
I should just say "pass."

I'm the next one to share,
so I tell a funny joke.
The class erupts in laughter,
but I wish I hadn't spoke.

My teacher glances at me
and gives me a stare.
She's disappointed and angry.
That is so unfair!

My teacher isn't happy
and tells me, "Please sit!"
The students all laugh,
but I'm ready to quit.

My face gets all hot,
turns a bright shade of red.
I'm embarrassed and wish
I had watched what I said.

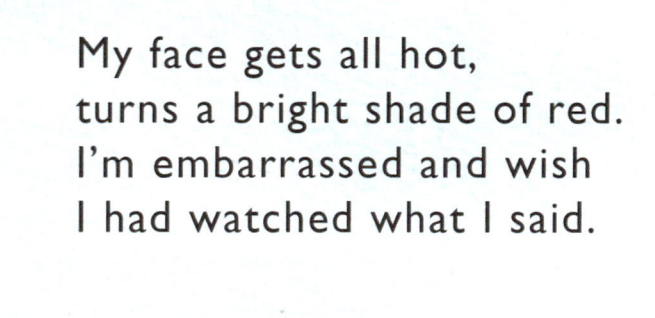

It's time to eat snack!
I go sit with my friend.

A nice break in the day
that just needs to end.

I find a quiet spot to read with zero distraction. Let's see if I can do something without a reaction.

I stare at the pages
with no clue what I've read.

So I write down a note,
and guess what it said?

My teacher doesn't like me, which is just so unfair.

She doesn't think I'm funny. She doesn't even care.

I take the note that I wrote,
and pass it around.

My teacher then finds it,
picks it up off the ground.

We line up for lunch,
my favorite part of the day.

But my teacher says to me,
"I need you to stay."

A mix of emotions
swim 'round in my head.

Could this day be any worse?
Now I won't even get fed.

My friends head to lunch while I stay in class.

I wait for my teacher, watching time quickly pass.

She comes back to the room, and I wish I could hide.

She said she found my note with the message inside.

I try not to cry.
I feel a lump in my throat.

I share how I feel,
and why I wrote what I wrote.

My teacher gives me a hug,
smiling from ear to ear.
She said, "Of course, I like you!
Please let that be clear!"

"It's my job as your teacher to take care of the class."
"If you're loud and disruptive, there is no free pass."

"If you need extra help
or a quiet space to be,

go move around the room
or ask to see me."

"If you struggle with lessons in math, reading, or writing,

come ask me for help. I'll be there for guiding."

"Breaks in the day
help to get your sillies out."

"Take a walk or a lap,
it helps to move about!"

"Let's plan time during the day just to work one on one!"

"I think working together will make school more fun."

I agree to our plan.
Help is just what I need.

Working hard and listening
will help me succeed.

www.ingramcontent.com/pod-product-compliance
Lightning Source LLC
Chambersburg PA
CBRC091204010526
44107CB00021B/1243